LESSONS from the WOLVERINE

Lessons from the Wolverine

Barry Lopez

Illustrations by Tom Pohrt

The University of Georgia Press
Athens and London

Published by the University of Georgia Press
Athens, Georgia 30602
Copyright © 1997 by Barry Holstun Lopez and Tom Pohrt
"Lessons from the Wolverine" copyright © 1994 by Barry
Holstun Lopez
Illustrations copyright © 1997 by Tom Pohrt

"Lessons from the Wolverine" is from *Field Notes: The Grace Note of
the Canyon Wren*, by Barry Lopez, published by Alfred A. Knopf
in 1994. It is reprinted by arrangement with the publisher.

Designed by David Bullen
Set in Perpetua with La Bamba display

The paper in this book meets the guidelines for permanence
and durability of the Committee on Production Guidelines for
Book Longevity of the Council on Library Resources.

Printed in Korea by Sung In Printing America, Inc.

01 00 99 98 97 C 5 4 3 2 1

Library of Congress Cataloging in Publication Data
Lopez, Barry Holstun, 1945–
Lessons from the wolverine / by Barry Lopez ; illustrations by
Tom Pohrt.
p.   cm.
ISBN 0-8203-1927-9 (alk. paper)
1. Wolverine——Fiction. I. Title.
PS3562.067L47   1997
813'.54——dc21   96-54705

British Library Cataloging in Publication Data available

Published simultaneously in Canada by Key Porter Books,
Toronto, Ontario

IN THE Ruby Mountains, where the Sanumavik River heads, there is supposed to be living now, and for as far back as memory can go, a family of wolverine. I first learned about them in an offhand way, so often the case with information like this, which turns up in a remote village and subsequently proves startling or strange.

One evening I was playing catch with a boy named Narvalaq, a boy of twelve in a village on the Koanik River, part of the Sanumavik drainage. I missed a throw and had to retrieve the ball from the river. It landed in shallow water trickling over a point bar, beautiful cobbles — reds, grays, greens, browns. Walking back, I moved slowly, stooped over, studying rocks that had been polished by the river and now were shining in the late evening light, each one bright as an animal's eye.

Narvalaq came up and said, "Wolverine, up at Caribou Caught by the Head Creek, they walk along like that. That's how you know it's them."

I nodded. I wanted to think it over, but right away I was interested in what he had to say. First I believed he meant that wolverine living at that place looked very closely at stones or at other things in the river, that they studied things more than other wolverines do. But I learned later in a conversation with Elisha Atnah, Narvalaq's father, that they just like to walk in the shallows. When these Caribou-Caught-by-the-Head wolverine are traveling alongside water they like to walk in it.

"Like you did that time," said Elisha.

The village where I was told this is called Eedaqna. A year after it happened I got back to Eedaqna—but perhaps I should tell you a little about myself first, so you will understand more about this story. I grew up in the West Indies, Antigua, around there. We lost my mother in a hurricane, big flood. In 1974, when I was eight,

we moved to Tennessee, my father and I. He taught mathematics at Union University. I began walking in the hills then, looking at animals. I liked being near them. In 1978 my father died and I went to northern Alberta to live with his brother. I tried to get the knack of going to school when I lived there, but I couldn't. I liked to walk around on the prairie, along the creeks. One thing I did then was to fly falcons. I liked being out with them, watching them circle over-head, getting a sense of the country I couldn't get. But it was hard keeping them in cages. I couldn't keep it up.

I ended up working on prop planes in Edmonton when I was eighteen, which I got very good at. I've had good jobs all along. Every time I left one — Peace River, Fort Smith, Yellowknife — I went farther north. In 1989 I moved to Kaktovik, where I still am. I haven't started a family yet, which is all right with me, but my friends in the coastal villages and up in the Brooks Range don't like it. They don't talk to me quite as much because I don't have a family. No children. They believe it's strange. But they have strangeness in their own lives.

I didn't forget what Narvalaq said. I thought it was something to know, what he had said about the wolverine. So the first time I could I went back to Eedaqna, when a Cessna 206 crashed there. Maybe someone would tell me something more. I talked to an old man working with me on the plane, Abraham Roosevelt, trying to move the conversation around to wolverines up on the Sanumavik. (I don't know another way with them except backing into it.) First, I said I might move to Eedaqna. Maybe, he said. I said I might trap in the winter, then go north to Kaktovik in summer to work on planes. He said maybe I would do that. Then I said if I trapped, I'd want to trap where no one else was, even if I had to travel a long way every day to my trapline. He said that might be good. Where would I go? I asked. Lots of places to go, he said. What about the Ruby Mountains, I said, up there at the head

of the Sanumavik, was that too far? That's not a good place, he said, not too good. Why? He looked at me for a moment then went back to work on one of the carburetors. He talked about one family that had lost a lot when this plane went down. Everyone was trying to help them now. Later, he said to me, "Wolverine that live up that way, Sanumavik River, they don't like it when people trap. They don't have that up there."

That conversation, when I first learned how those wolverine felt, happened in the spring of 1990. The following winter I met a woman named Dora Kahvinook living in Kaktovik, but who was from Eedaqna. She took a liking to me, and I liked her, too. She told me some stories that were unusual for her to have, hunting stories about her two brothers and her father. I asked if her father or her brothers had ever gone hunting in the upper Sanumavik. She said no. I said two people in Eedaqna had told me that the wolverine that lived up there didn't like people coming up. She said she didn't know, but, yes, that's what people said.

That winter I dreamed four times about wolverine. I decided I was going to go up there when spring came, regardless. I've never been able to learn what I want to know about animals from books or looking at television. I have to walk around near them, be in places where they are. This was the heart of the trouble that I had in school. Many of the stories that should have been told about animals, about how they live, their different ways, were never told. I don't know what the stories were, but when I walked in the woods or out on the prairie or in the mountains, I could feel the boundaries of those stories. I knew they were there, the way you know fish are in a river. This knowledge was what I wanted, and the only way I had gotten it was to go out and look for it. To be near animals until they showed you something that you didn't imagine or you hadn't seen or heard.

In June I went back to Eedaqna and asked

Elisha Atnah if he would travel with me. I told him I had felt the wolverine up on the Sanumavik River pulling on me over the winter. They didn't leave me alone. He listened and a few days later he said he would go with me. We traveled down the Koanik and then up the Sanumavik. It was a long way and we walked, we didn't take three-wheelers. Elisha said it would be better to walk. We walked for three days. In the evening, I asked Elisha questions.

"How many families of wolverine live up there?"

"Just that one. But it's a big family, they have been up there as long as anyone remembers. That's all their country."

"Are they different from other wolverine, like ones living over on Sadlerochit?"

"Wolverines are all different. Each family, different."

After a while he came back to this. He said, "Wolverines have culture, same as people do, but they all look the same to some people because they carry it in their heads. That's how all animals are different. Almost all their culture — I think that's the word I mean — it's inside their heads."

"You mean tools, drums, winter clothing — things like that?"

"That's right. Everything they need — stories, which way to travel, a way to understand the world — that's all in their heads. Sometimes you will find a bed they have made, or a little house, or maybe where they have made marks on the ground for dancing. You might sometime see a fox riding a piece of wood down a river where he is going. But you don't see many things like that. Their winter clothes — they just come out from inside them."

"Which story is the one that tells a person not to set a trapline in this country we are going to?"

"One time, long time ago, before my father can remember, we trapped in that country. Some marten and lynx. River otter. Mink and short-tailed weasel. For some reason, no one trapped wolves there. We left wolves alone but we looked

really hard for wolverine. My father's uncle, Tusamik, he belonged to that place then, and his youngest boy, he started setting every kind of trap along one creek. Moon Hiding the Daylight Creek. He found a caribou there, pretty much finished up, and he set traps around it. He didn't come back until five days later, maybe — too many days. He didn't understand, that country was very generous to us. He had caught a wolverine, one front foot, one back foot." Here, Elisha stood up and showed me how the wolverine was stretched out. "But the wolverine, she was standing on top of a wolf! She had gotten the life out of him. Killed him. And there was also blood from another wolf in the snow. Tusamik's boy studied what had happened, each animal's marks. The wolverine had first been caught by a front foot. Then the two wolves had come along. That caribou meat was there, but for some reason they wanted the life in that wolverine, so they tried to get it. They came at her at the same time from two directions. The wolverine, she killed the first wolf right away—and all the time she was jumping around with that trap on her foot. Then she stepped in the second trap, with her back foot, and she couldn't move very much. But she had hurt that other wolf already. It went away. The boy thought it all happened two days, maybe, before he got there.

"The wolverine was angry. She told the boy it was over, wolverines were not going to do this anymore. The boy said he was sorry, but the wolverine said no, there won't be any more trapping for a while. Too many days waiting for him.

"So, we don't trap any animals there now. We don't go up there too much."

WE WENT away from the Sanumavik River the next day, up Caribou Caught by the Head Creek. When we got to a place where the tundra was hilly and open, only a few trees, willows, around, Elisha said he was going to leave.

He told me to just sit there and wait. In the afternoon I saw two wolverine at the crest of a hill. They came down close to the creek where I was and lay down in the sunshine on the far side and went to sleep. I had backed up against some rocks that were warm from the sun and I went to sleep, too. I began dreaming about the wolverines. It was night. I saw the two of them lying on their backs on the side of the hill. They were talking. They motioned for me to come over and lie down next to them. I did. It was dark all over the tundra. They were talking about the stars.

"You have to pay attention," one of them said. "We're going to show you something."

I looked up into the sky and along one edge of the Milky Way I could see it was different. The stars were quivering in a pattern along that edge. It was like water running over a shallows in the sunshine.

"Look in there," said the other wolverine. "Look right in there."

I looked into the pattern. I was a bird then,

looking down like an osprey, flying high over the water, a river moving across the tundra. I could see many things moving in the current. Fish. Under the water I saw shells, sand, the colors of Antigua. Then leaves turning in the current, like they did in the Hatchie in Tennessee in the fall. One leaf was my father's face. Other people. Then the face of a wild dog, a crazy animal, sick. I remember my father fighting in the woods with that dog. Then for a long time leaves—the faces of animals I had seen in the woods in Tennessee and away in Alberta. The leaves were many colors and shapes. Tulip trees and poplars. Some faces, some animals, I remembered. I felt sad and tried to pull my eyes away but I couldn't. I started to remember them all, every one of those animals.

"I'm afraid," I said. "I want to get down, come down to the ground now." But nothing happened.

"Keep going," said one of the wolverines.

Looking upriver, the water was green.

27

Looking the other way, downriver, it was bluer. Below me it was all transparent. Leaves tumbling there. The river spilled over a line of black mountains far away, through a dark blue sky. A wind was blowing and I was cold. I wanted to get down. Then I saw myself below, looking up, shading my eyes with the heavy glove, the jesses in my other hand. I was waving.

"This is our power," said one of the wolverines.

Where I was looking, in still water, the faces were trembling like aspen leaves in a wind. Animals I recognized—black bear, snapping turtle, lark sparrow, monarch butterfly, corn snake, wolf spider, porcupine, yellow-shafted flicker, muskellunge—memories of those days. Trembling like leaves on a branch. A curtain of willow leaves, through which sunlight blinked. I heard my heart beat, regular, loud. I lay on the ground, my back sideways against warm rocks. I was looking out through river willows at a hillside. The wolverines weren't there anymore.

I sat up and looked around for Elisha. He wasn't there either. I waded the creek. Where the wolverine had been the grass was pressed down but there were no tracks. I stood there for a long time, watching the sky, the hills, all around.

From where I stood I could see across to where Elisha had left me, by rocks that were dotted with bright orange and yellow lichen. On one of the rocks I could see something. I crossed back over and walked up to it. It was a willow stick, about two feet long and curved like a small bow. It had been carved to look like a wolverine running, raising its back in that strange way they have when they are hurrying along. Tied around the neck was a string of ten wolverine claws. It looked too strong to pick up. I left it on the rock and sat down to wait for Elisha.

After a while I picked up the wolverine stick and held it in my lap. Elisha came from a direction I wasn't looking, from the Sanumavik River. We went back there and camped. He said the

claws were from the left front foot and the right rear foot of a wolverine. Female, he said. I told him about seeing the animals from my past. I felt them all around. I felt I was carrying something in my head that hadn't been there before. He said he was glad.

Elisha said he didn't know what the stick animal meant. He told me to carry it, not to put it inside my pack. He said we could ask someone when we got back to Eedaqna.